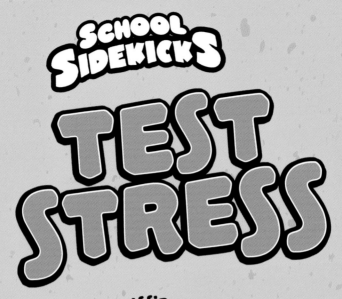

# SCHOOL SIDEKICKS
# TEST STRESS

by Molly Beth Griffin
illustrated by Mike Deas

PICTURE WINDOW BOOKS
a capstone imprint

# TABLE OF CONTENTS

# SCHOOL SIDEKICKS

**These five friends live within the walls, nooks, and crannies of an elementary school. They learn alongside kids every day, even though the kids don't see them!**

## STELLA

Stella is a mouse. She loves her friends. She also loves children and school! She came into the school on a cold winter day. She knew it would be her home forever. Her favorite subjects are social studies and music. She is always excited for a new day.

## BO

Bo is a parakeet. He is a classroom pet. The friends let him out of his cage so they can play together. Bo loves to read. He goes home with his teacher on weekends, but he always comes back to school to see his friends.

# DELILAH

Delilah is a spider. She has always lived in the corners of the school. She is so small the children never notice her, but she is very smart. Delilah loves math and computers and hates the broom.

# NICO

Nico is a toad. He used to be a classroom pet. A child forgot to put him back into his tank one day. Now he lives with his friends. The whole school is his home! He can be grumpy, but he loves science and art. Since Nico doesn't have fingers, he paints with his toes!

# GOLDIE

Goldie is a goldfish. She is very wise. The friends ask her questions when they have a big choice to make. She gives good advice and lives in the media center.

# THE JITTERS

"My stomach hurts," said Stella the Mouse.

Her friends nodded. They felt kind of sick too. Nico the Toad paced. Delilah the Spider's legs drummed—all eight of them. Bo the Parakeet hid in his cage with a big book.

All weekend the friends had been nervous. Now it was Sunday. Testing week began tomorrow!

Stella, Nico, Delilah, and Bo had been learning along with the children for months. Now they were going to take the tests with them too.

Their brains were ready. But their bodies were not.

"How will I do my best when I don't feel my best?" Stella asked.

She rubbed her stomach.

"Let's go ask Goldie," said Nico.

"She'll know what to do," Delilah agreed. "Come on, Bo."

The friends went to Goldie the Goldfish whenever they had a problem. She lived in the media center. She was very wise. She would know how to help with this test stress.

"Goldie, will we do okay on our tests?" Stella squeaked.

Goldie swam in a circle.

"Blub," she said.

One blub meant yes. Two blubs meant no. At least that's what the friends thought she meant.

Nico smiled a small smile.

"We WILL do okay," he said.

"Goldie believes in us," said Delilah.

"But Goldie, are we really ready to take the tests?" Stella asked. Her stomach still hurt.

"Blub, blub," said Goldie.

"No! Did you just say no?"

Nico asked.

Goldie wiggled her fins.

"She's right," Stella told her friends. "My brain feels ready, but my body does NOT."

"Well, how can we help our bodies?" asked Bo.

Goldie looked at each of the friends, one at a time.

"We each need to think of one thing our bodies might need," said Delilah.

"If we do all those things together, we'll be ready," said Bo.

Goldie swam in a circle.

"Blub," she said.

Yes!

# THE PLAN

The friends each came up with one idea for everyone to try.

"We have to get a good night's sleep tonight," said Stella. "Then we will be rested for tomorrow."

In the morning, Nico fed them a big, healthy breakfast. It had all the food groups.

"We need our strength," he said. "Good food will give us energy. And help us focus."

After breakfast, Delilah led them all in exercises. They did stretches and jumping jacks. Bo fell asleep stretching.

"We have to get the wiggles out of ALL our legs!" she said. "Then we'll be able to sit for the tests."

But they were still nervous. Even after a good sleep. Even after a healthy breakfast. Even after exercises. They still felt jittery and jumpy.

Finally, Bo showed them the big book he'd been reading all weekend.

"This is what we need to do," he said. "Take a deep breath. In . . . and out. And in . . . and out."

The breathing helped the friends feel calm.

"Think positive," said Bo. "That's what the book says."

The bell rang.

The friends rushed off to
sharpen their pencils. They settled
in and began their tests. Their
brains AND their bodies were
ready now.

# CELEBRATE!

The tests were hard. But the friends knew a lot. They knew even more than they realized!

They didn't know everything, of course. And sometimes they made mistakes. But they did their best. Trying felt good.

One time when Stella came to a very hard problem, her stomach suddenly hurt again. She started to sweat and felt a little dizzy.

Stella looked at the children. They were hard at work. They were trying their best.

Then she looked at her friends. They were hard at work too. Stella remembered how her friends believed in her.

She breathed in . . . and out. And in . . . and out.

"Think positive," she whispered. "Just try. It will be okay."

And it was.

On Friday, everybody was tired. But everybody was also very happy to be done. The friends were proud of the children and proud of themselves.

Then—SURPRISE! The teachers threw a dance party for the children in the gym. The friends went too! They stayed out of the way of all the dancing feet.

They snuck slices of pizza and sips of punch. But just a little. Stella did NOT want another tummy ache!

# TALK ABOUT IT

1. Everyone feels stressed or anxious at times. Talk about things that make you feel stressed.

2. How does your body react when you are feeling anxious? Are your reactions always the same?

3. Do you think staying positive helps relieve stress? Why or why not?

# WRITE ABOUT IT

1. Make a list of things you can do if you are feeling stressed. Look back in the story for some ideas.

2. Eating a healthy breakfast before a big test is important. Make a menu of a healthy breakfast. Be sure to include all the food groups.

3. Write a paragraph about what you do to celebrate after a stressful event.

# MOLLY BETH GRIFFIN

Molly Beth Griffin is a writing teacher at the Loft Literary Center in Minneapolis, Minnesota. She has written numerous picture books (including *Loon Baby* and *Rhoda's Rock Hunt*) and a YA novel *(Silhouette of a Sparrow)*. Molly loves reading and hiking in all kinds of weather. She lives in South Minneapolis with her partner and two kids.

# MIKE DEAS

Mike Deas is a cartoonist, illustrator, and graphic novelist. His love for illustrative storytelling comes from an early love of reading and drawing. Capilano College's Commercial Animation Program in Vancouver helped Mike fine-tune his drawing skills and imagination. Mike lives with his family on sunny Salt Spring Island, British Columbia, Canada.

# PLENTY OF SIDEKICK FUN!

School Sidekicks is published by
Picture Window Books, a Capstone Imprint
1710 Roe Crest Drive, North Mankato, Minnesota 56003
www.capstonepub.com

Library of Congress Cataloging-in-Publication Data
Names: Griffin, Molly Beth, author.
Title: Test stress / by Molly Beth Griffin.
Description: North Mankato, Minnesota : Picture Window Books, [2020]
Series: School sidekicks

Summary: Stella the Mouse, Nico the Toad, Delilah the Spider,
and Bo the Parakeet are nervous about testing week,
but by working together they get ready to do their best.

Identifiers: LCCN 2019006023| ISBN 9781515844198 (hardcover) |
ISBN 9781515844235 (ebook pdf)
Subjects: | CYAC: Test anxiety—Fiction. | Preparedness—Fiction.
|Friendship—Fiction. | Animals—Fiction. | Schools—Fiction.

Classification: LCC PZ7.G8813593 Tes 2019 |
DDC [E]—dc23 LC record available at https://lccn.loc.gov/2019006023

Designer: Ted Williams

Design elements: Shutterstock: AVA Bitter, design element throughout,
Oleksandr Rybitskiy, design element throughout

Printed and bound in the United States of America.
3443